So I'll see you in decade

As Young As Toddlers

Drift apart

A decade later

Things go wrong

The brothel

The tip off

The budge

Date gang violence

Meeting at the airport

See you in a decade regrets, and secretly works miracles

Rescues illness crime

The imposter

A decade passes

The anomaly

Sighting at the train station

Make a pact to find her again

The ending

AS YOUNG TODDLERS

In the beginning , young and youthful used to live in the same neighbourhood she used to own the shop D own the road by the library our families or now I call it as astray basked in riches and wealth everybody had their place in the main scene of things . II.   Moments I recall kissing behinds the tennis courts getting told off by our parents at the tennis club everybody trying too divine in reputation. beneath the attitude of keeping up appearance s and the young free spirits souls of kindred youth. III.   Back to that kiss our lips met we smiled then as if to peck and in my mind my soul had risen and aged as if I saw the future in her, to be my contentment and soul purpose and reason to live. under the stars on brisk October darkness contrasting low blue light my heart had even skipped a step at the very memories.

Drift apart

Years went by as we had ages category placement at school separated by class and distinction we were separated by the new way of life being in schools it wasn't the same memories fade distraction all I guess on how I'm growing up could like at my age still I didn't quite fit in always knew there was some entity missing like abandonment yet not of choice or of fault .

New faces some cool hip and fashionable sort then your rough edges I fit into both some days good other days well let not reoccur. Only seeing her occasionally weekends yet had new groups now a then a stranger I believed she was in fact wasn't my perception Memories. new attractions all the uncertainty she was still beautiful though her hazel eyes her intensive tender smile.

A DECADE later................

Stabbing police corruption

Waking up to the sound of arguing my step dad and foster mum arguing over me staying I manage to slip out the door take a half dazed distracted confused and grumbling stroll not inclined to understand and compute the last twelve minutes to find a moment Holding myself up against a red fire brick wall taking a breath resting my head on my arms in dismay . Suddenly A cry for help! Help! "please don't stab me I'll get the money ". Within that moment I realised I'd been in that moment before within an instant I grabbed a fallen piece of brick from the crooked wall and threw it at the window .I reasoned with the aggressors calling up I'm calling the police please let me pay the money leave and get out of here the boys exited a dream cry of sorrowfully pain the culprits fled I got to the girl lying on the floor date drugged bleeding she was shivering uncalm and scared she answered don't hurt me I took my hood or bandana lightly pressured the wound assuring her she be safe the services were on their way she what if they came back I told her they have to kill me first as I lay beside her holding the wound as I looked into her eyes that moment she peered up at me and smiled in shock my feelings went all soft I recognised her wondering feeling deep deep affection before I realised the police had arrived .

I told them u had two stabbers on the loose she replied in facetious manner, you don't tell me what to do.

The ambulance arrived and helped carry her down the flight of steps And that was the last I saw of her in the heat blue flashing lights how many things could go wrong in a few moments still disturbed by my own grievance horrified and still left alone that feeling I had the shock still awaking from an uneasy deep dark sleep. I venture back home an explain the goings on to find the argument in full heat still I then get the degree on how I should sort my act out.

Things go wrong

Remittances when Time goes by but losing my mind patient holding on to the memories of that feeling I couldn't talk like anything people had say was already said a thousand times again a thousand time over like a thousand times again and feeling it would be a thousand times again I'm struck by silence like I had left my body and mind and was a being of the equilibrium the limbo everything gave me a harmful spirit like my spirit was trapped in a valley of stinging nettles a radiation of pain I stayed silent like I heard it all before every very word length me I'd been here time and time again heard every every word I was trapped in the memories like in limbo away from the reality it was like the whole world revolving around me I was the centre like a weight and the world revolves in circles lost in the equilibrium my memories of her trapped inside like I was living in spirit my feeling like a secret smile holding onto the very feelings of Elation and desire of my memories of her .

The brothel boy raped hypnotised on the escape

Years went by and Time got normal some youthful life recovery was the reason for my new outlook on life I felt vibrant healthy well off I could enjoy the sunshine summers were free from problems I could live drink and hang out in the gardens by the river with friends getting along in till one afternoon a table of drinkers that I had not seen before I sat down joined the conversation" jog off " the women said I had recognised her with a cautious gut feeling we bantered And it just do happened that she was a school teacher and asked if I'd come to her school with a guitar to show off and play for the kids I took her number and arranged the day .any way little did I know what was about to unfold I was being groomed she insisted me in and began the fun and games . Time went by and my suspicions became a problem I found myself drugged and unable to leave the comfort of my wasted state. I then fell into a deep subconscious state then women and men were having sex with me in my consciousness they were feeding me with poison s I didn't know about in an out of consciousness I fell not knowing who was the problem who they were and why this was happening . Lust filled fantasies as I came round I found myself trapped in the limbo of uncertainty and a none existing self-control of volatile outburst of aggression and uncontrollable psychosis ,I knew I had to leave only to find a conspiracy when the police turned up and arrested me taking me back to my home jailed and released only to find my house ransacked boarded up with nowhere to go this was the second time that year I had to move due to conflict smashed windows from killers hustled by the care team that I had to go and do what they say so despair and anxiety kicked in do I think quick with cocaine trafficking rinks on my tail a corrupt police force looming the only way was to escape in my collective consciousness I declare a bid to escape the UK for breather .

The tip off

So I head to the city in great haste ducking and diving I find a steady rock bar and stop and slump over a pint glass with slouching dismay wait on my shoulders I couldn't find the mind set to talk around and in shock I was however losing the will to live again my peace was distributed the year I had list jobs lost courses Sabatier s the drama conflict I still was nothing and no one with nothing and no one still with hope youth on my side I wasn't quite able to loose yet my senses looked into the future like a third eye it felt mythic but full of positive vibrations something was worth the direction I was heading in something reminded me a benevolent friend told me once "theirs light at the end of the tunnel without a doubt if not I'll have to come again renew you " . So, I thought new life start again and hope for the best. As then I was approached by a women who had been bickering with her friends across the bar glancing over she said something I was too deep in thought to realise what she said she left I told her I was leaving soon so I left quite quickly . I prepared the rest of the cash as took to my hotel room to find a flight to my new life.

The very next morning I arose to a rainy Damp morning set off to the airport busy and queuing into the secure hindered passage way to collect my boarding tickets and check in the queue was just enough to wait I felt self-conscious as I like to call it think stair and in the corner of my eye I noticed the flight attendant at the desk I looked up and I caught her eyes gleaming at me the precisely the moment

As if she looked at me in compassion with that smile nose Dipped with that bashful sincerity and I started to see the beginning of the tunnel." hey trouble ". Her cheeks rising, I replied hey have we met before rather taken back confused she replied I used to know you when you were younger but haven't seen you in a long time.

I replied with a smile on my face u know what I recognise you she said you helped me out once I replied I've helped a lot of people to be honest the tragedies id been through I'd blocked out blacked out of my mind even though that feeling I hadn't felt for a decade hadn't computed was really just becoming a sensation I instantly put a lid on I'd bottle it up do much the very hint of that emotion again I had a new mind set new ego even though my conscious knew I was wrong denying my past the write to affect my conscious being to bring up thoughts and regret of shame dismay and anguish.

But God how great it was I felt I felt responsible compassionate and flattered I felt a sense of pride there was something so special I was wondering a mutual feeling of compassion sincerity in her radiant feminine pout as she took a step back and gazed in insecurity Confusion I felt a sullen shame realising I can't embrace my moments that I dream of that I wish for , not that I realised that at the time but that was the first inclination that the decade to come .

I then said maybe see you again sometimes she replied I'm on the flight your help on.

I then took a walk through customs the role line to get through no hindrance I might add the soulful wait in the waiting room back to thinking of what I'd just been threw feeling beat and ashamed earning sensation of trying to stop myself from crying keeping my libido from crashing into oblivion I took a breath and hyperventilating I was interrupted there was a call over the announcement speakers calling my name the corrupt enemies had realised I was making an escape they were on my tail I ducked and dived changing my appearance dressing in the toilets edging my way threw to my gate as my gate was announced open .

Getting anxious at the gate surrendering my boarding pass

Fingers crossed I get threw as walked the jetty to board the plane

I walked past the stewardesses and took my seat left hand side row Isle seat row 19.

Feeling anxious and nervous about whether the flight would take off before anymore drama s the flight attendant catching my eye made a quite extreme launch towards me saying hi do you remember me

 said yes u look familiar gently recalling I'm from or used be from and said she thought she'd recognised me didn't quite place her there and then still dazed and confused I humoured quite realising she was the love of my life but I felt overwhelmed and flattered the way she suddenly got friendly with a huge smile I felt about a billion times better and when I least expected it too .

So, an hour or two into the flight the stewardess s were busy serving alcohol a nice young gentleman served me ,as of that moment the lady who approached me looked rather agitated and stressed out

I then took a moment got up of my seat and followed her to the toilet cubicles I waited and spoke to her and said you know it's wonderful to see you again it's sort of coming back to me our eyes met our heads Dipped and there was definitely that feeling that feeling that hadn't existed in me for years like it was my first breath

Like a connection as my heart beat skipped q step she then looked down after a moment of silence hey some advice the place your going too is full of those people and corrupt circle be careful because I heard they were out to get you they've even bullied me .

Then very elegantly walked off back to her duties

The flight procedures exit manoeuvre and seat belt secure check list

We eventually came to our descent over our destination landed smoothly and I walked past and said well sparks flew in jest she became quite bashful I walked down the step s to the great ground and a voice said hey would you want to hang around for a bit so I did people left and I stuck around as it was the lady's first flight as a member of staff will you take a picture of me on the landing gear

I said yes took the camera this dainty little pink pro new modern digital cam with a silver click smile elegantly my lady she looked sorrowfully at me with the most intense frown with cheeks Raised

half happy half confused bashful with that daze I hadn't quite placed or remembered yet I made her smile and applauded her first Flight she did perk up then she even got a stair lift onto the wing and sat like a sassy lady crossed legged I took more photos of her she said would you like to stay with us from this moment I have no idea why I did what I did I had to go across several islands to get to my destination so I said I sort of got to go even though my feelings dropped the further away I got from her and I walked away tired and about to embark on a long treck even I was ignoring the fact that I really did want to stay but the mind set of the destination and eagerness to reach my destination collecting my luggage from the parasol and set on my way now stupidly I reached my destination sat for no longer than two minutes realised who it was and that I should go back I fell in love at the very thought of who it was   I can't believe I walked away so I decided to go back to find her . That moment.

The bugder

A young girl Italian girl I thought came in slender thin tiny to man of my size excusee sir would you say how do you say will you go out with me I returned the question and said no how old are you with parents I got agitated thinking this was offensive too me

I shouted good heaven girl not in million years she got offensive I was suspicious this was the crime rink I was messing with. She left came back with a beer saying was a peace offering I thought nothing of it and relaxed sipping my beer back into thought of my new revelation of the lady I once knew. I got up and suddenly felt faint faint as can be I then lay to the ground .what had occurred meanwhile behind my back was the most unsavoury plot of destruction about to unfold just like what I was informed about I had indeed been spiked and was surrounded by people perhaps I wouldn't have let near me my own very fault for walking away .

The girl in fact had been sent to set me up for a ligation or for baiting me into situations that I'd been through before . The corrupt

officers were all over me using lies deceitful cruel intentional defective crime.

Date rape / and gang violence

Behind my back the previous meditated gangs turned up one by other corners of each street the dark side roads of the calle

With knives guns bats they started striping me down having sex with me taking my excrement kicking slapping me punching me putting their hands down my throat I slipped in and out of consciousness people really really went there distance realising the feelings even year later being violated makes me physically sick
.

Then Local dude is knowing baseball batted the woman the very same women from the police force years before people started to fight

The Guardia civil were compassionate helping the riot I had to go to hospital half into a comatose state of bruises and damaged libido

Nothing that I didn't know before just with sullen warmth that I had indeed want to sink into I was now indeed somewhere lost in the equilibrium I didn't really want to regain consciousness as it was bliss my feeling s was in fact a seventh heaven a heaven so hidden in my subconscious it tells me she's their too , but as I come round to wake hit with this sudden pain of guilt anguish and regret she to be nowhere in site that reality that nobody knows without nothing and no one the let down the feeling of being impaired your thoughts of where and why and rationality go out the window feeling at a kiss not knowing what for . Waking up in a placebo base reality like nothing had happened people acting close to me the very touch the sickness and collapse of my very nerve system shut down with sullen hallucinations of crime s of horror like there was urgency but. Couldn't physically move I cringed with fear feeling displaced and anxious. Had to leave and my memory faded, and the very feeling of destiny was a dark long distance to find myself again.

The escape wasn't the best planned affair realising I had to make it away into another circle as they could have traced me back to home, I had to use a place of collective conscience so injured and burnt

after a walk and a knight in the desert I called ambulance on the decent to the airport UK bound no passport just a warrant I had to leave obliviously so straight through customs and Into an accident emergency ward I had beat the following.

The cold freezing winter storms in the brisk darkness of the UK   I was released knowing where I was, I made my way to the mountains harbour in comfort just disgraced and discreet in a public Resort.

meeting in the airport after coffee chips

I can't stop thinking about the lady stewardess it seem s well getting back to philosophy or famous quotes if first you don't succeed yet try and try again so I completely completely tried to contact her so I went to the airport again on the off chance she was their I first went to church and made a prayer to help me have strength to be as honest and genuine to tell her without manipulating that I really really really want to be with her and my life some how incomplete without her in my life I had nothing going for me I was again jobless workless list and a t a cross roads something deep inside me is talk ng me so strong that somehow done reason she was my reason to live and if as she don't love me I lose everything myself my mind almost like my life was just for her like I owe her every breath every day every star in the sky every cloud rain drop you know I mean deep . I found her straight away she said I'll meet you in forty-five minutes on my break before I fly

We sat down I ate chips and we chatted she still was with the guy who asked her out and life was good do I then didn't mention I had a ring in my pocket and didn't tell her what I really meant to say so I turned on my ego and said is there any chance of being friends and be like pen pals she's said I'm about to get into a serious relationship and I'm a bit trouble s o she said perhaps this is the last time we should speak because it's too intense I smiled behind my wall of front and ego I took a sorrowful breath and said well I'll see you in s decade IL come find you in ten years and see if it ok because your someone I want to check in with for one reason I'm

attracted to you I don't know why but do me the justice she said no hat can't happen no no I frowned she looked into my eyes with puppy dog eyes stood up and gave me a hug I kissed her cheek and let her go .

She walked down her terminal as I left the airport and said to herself if he comes back in a decade, I think how o romantic too herself lovely.

See you in decade

Regrets it secretly Works miracles

So, he sees you from afar and loves you from. Distance well what was said in Krishna any way so I realised I missed my chance she chose her life I walked away from I was happy for her and pleased to see her yet deep inside how much you can lose in a moment

Well yeah life revolves in circles what goes around comes around although I don't like stereo type in any way well that's what happened so I still love her in a special way I say to myself ok just because I'm not eligible at this moment and at a cross roads I still have feelings of a major priority what don't I make myself the best I can be if I can use all my heart suddenly I felt strength lion heart in a word of exhilarating proportion . This was trouble!

All of then a sudden walk and aspiration I walked a new walk into town the city lights the solitude but the strength of Gallagher into what was known as the first city slicker horror movie a man being beat and assaulted by thugs bleeding thick venous bleeding I fought the men off and called an ambulance I then walked off into the night not acknowledge the scene before completely new to the bar I propped myself into a pint seconds later it kicks off suddenly a bar fight was taken outside I felt an angelic presence through me and stood bolt upright wings thrusted threw me like graceful but vigilance.

Creates s rescues illness crime

So back to the crime wave the crime wave seemed fierce

And fully at large yet I still took on board the philosophy that life is for living and must have a creative outlet do happens in s musician

Not bragging but quite famous u know worked with bands and written for some quite incredible artists I'm mean really and some movies not of the adult kind I'm inspired by romance conflict And life I guess not willing or ever wished to be world famous or dreamed of it yet it was all around me my alternate ego I was however creative and love nothing more to express my feelings and emotions and my dream regularly searching for someone I love an old friend or someone who is trust worthy to I suspospe get some sympathy some affection some love do u know what it makes me content even in my darkest lonely state like I found it says in the Bible in your anger do not sin when you are in your bed s search your hearts and be silence and with that I'm happy even in my solitude it my special place and most secret . Away from the incredible forces of the crime rink u know identity frauds surveillance set ups framing using against sabotage all the naughty perversion trafficking fraud you get jist now I can't believe I deserved all this but however growing up and realising that it

wasn't just life it was completely aimed at me I was a survivor victim witness even to any of the above sadism any human rights Science and a pact and plot too hurt my family and plot to take some people dear to me away and leave me lonely   The likes of framing using asylums very twisted and well organised tactical and the opposition deceptive and accurate even so much that it was biblical catching a heroically interventions on stabbings fights again it was all dangerous challenging what I knew of a simple life was no longer taking injuries losing some winning some it was a hard way I had to keep solitude use wit fend and survive my youth disappearing I didn't get a life I had to change my location each and every time a new place a new beginning in till it found me again   laws getting confused some help on the way some mistakes you know I was slowly changing a becoming a monster destructive nature again walking away from socialism live and friends scared for people I

love scared to commit gun fights hustling no time to settle no time just the trouble and allegations following me the rumours through the lines.

The imposter

So I walked into a pub after gun battles and some serious upset with s girl I used to know down the coast getting into problems wells as always so I think of convenient place to stay tired thinking it would be idiotic to stay outside so I approach the hills where usually I could get s chilled out environment . Now funny how sometimes you can approach an old friend and realise it was someone who looked the same well what happened next was either the most stupid or the best mistake I had made. I walked to the hills hotel and got a room for the night noticeable you the untrained ear but there was an open mic night I showered took out my smart night ware and proceeded to do a show and participate in the show I did a song and started chatting to a girl in the lounge " hey do I recognise you as he said maybe not sure I said you remind me of somebody a lady I used to know I thought it was her at first but by god she was good looking I thought first after being ripped off about this location knowing over three or four now look alike and an identity make up character of the lady who helped me thus was intense I prudently asked her what she does and for her number we chatted it was easy we connected we had fun u know really look back and all my worries from the last twenty four hours were ok now I felt warm enlightened she then grabbed my hand and invited me back a he had a gorgeous Siamese kitten he didn't like me s first but eventually he came round we talked about that she needed a job lost in the moment I mentioned to her that what about an air hostess obviously on my mind because I thought about her ? But really could I he be getting what I always wanted an amazing girlfriend. She then applied for the job and got it we hung out and she told me not to answer the door to anybody. Hours later there was knock at the door

A decade passes

A decade passes it had its ups and downs some success possess but I seem to come through it peachy on the other side I was a changed new man wise to life with the good intentions I started with were now a reality I was a super star with ambitions under my belt and a closer understanding of accomplishment yet not finished still single looking at the brighter side of life I had some pride and only the memories of the failed damaged my self-esteem I had learned to forgive myself. So, I had blocked out memories trainers' mistakes and was now an adult and adult who had made strict rules for myself and an idea of the man I want to be.

All the air was clear and was indeed recovered and in remission of my past my path with a clear vision if the future well ahead the time I had dreaded were now a distant reality.

All of coming to a conclusion I was now s bachelor prepared for a relationship no naughty affairs but well u know true love.

As I thought that an old photograph appeared to me that I had took of an old acquaintance somebody I had fell in love with time and time before again she had suddenly entered my mind I contacted her and we began to speak to each other again I did try to stop myself contacting her as memories were flooding back yet my heart and now strongly beating we began to speak again . Again, only one person on earth made me feel that way yes it was ....

I became happy instantly I asked her out on a date straight away even though I was preoccupied with life at that time it was great to be in contact again. Searching to try track her down

The anomaly.

My true feeling burning with passion and desire my spiritual rituals

And angelic astronomy embraced my passion I needed a sign then my feeling warmed and my hand s cupped a clenching of my wedding gift finger like if I tried to let go it suddenly would appear back like I was in and out if a realm happy yet missing her from a distance I cupped my hand and made a heart shape with my thumb and index finger the sun Shone I saw my heart cupped hand I peered at my shadow then the reflection in the window and then a heart shaped cloud in the sky even the gods were shining glorious gold sunsets and sunrises the sir was clear and fresh .

Sighting at the train station

At the crowded platform something she used to say popped into my mind on how she has to take her hat off at public transports I glanced and in the distance I thought my caught site of her a body and back swell through the crowds as they were boarding the train my heart raced at the thought nerves set in bracing me to freeze still .

The train was too full to board the same carriage, so I boarded and set off to the airport about three carriages up towards the front.

Joy energy lost her waiting in crowded station to airport

Rosalina get to know me waiting in airport curious with a watchful eye of a charity fund aid worker casually.

Sitting wondering why I keep arriving day after day curious to why I sit people watching like watching a memory as I'm Sat at airport she s on my mind watching and waiting seeing images of family's hugging say good bye or seeing each other after being a world apart, yet still no sign of her Feelings of anguish doubt deep in thought sense of benevolence

Being around her territory life with memories longing to see if we speak again or if she's still here available family? Increasing my chances of seeing her. Do what your heart tells

 Wondering watching waiting She feels a senses my presence in her heart somehow She's been informed or questioned on the matter Standoffish but senses the importance like the thought of a past memory turning into a Happy ending walking up the snail trail up the hill dreams of Getting engaged and Waits after not being able to find her but's into look alike memories of where we've been together I wait in anticipation.

 I finally give up and feel low about it I thought if I fall in love again, she could get hurt like the rest so bowing my head in shame after the prank or wishing she didn't get hurt

Make a pact to find her again

End up meeting her at a restaurant and her dating me lent feeling down years later when we were older it was so happy, she recognised me did and dated I've always thought about you "it was so intense ".

After the imposter striking again after more tragedies murder mayhem

The ending

    Memories growing weak and losing the very thought objective

so, he saddens and stairs into is heart longingly

With disaster in the he world things go aria like before

But a girl I'd been talking to comforted me at the bar

In a new location when I ran away to a coastal retreat lived in the community

Met loads of locals in the community

Every time I was saddened, she supports

make it look appear to be a new girl tanned lark black hair 2Hugs

comfort s and supports his shows

the twist?! She actually is the one he fell in love with all along without

Realising it / she had changed her identity.

(It was her.)

He changed his name to Benjamin and she had changed

Her name to Lucy

Benjamin with enough savings and Lucy lucky too

They brought a cottage got married in the local church

Not really initiating their past Ben and Lucy lived happily they were do much in love forever In The moment.

Ever after.